KIWI
CANNOT REACH!

DISCARD

WRITTEN AND ILLUSTRATED
BY JASON THARP

Ready-to-Read

Simon Spotlight
New York   London   Toronto   Sydney   New Delhi

To all the Kiwis out there,
keep reaching for those dreams!
I believe in you.

SIMON SPOTLIGHT

An imprint of Simon & Schuster Children's Publishing Division

1230 Avenue of the Americas, New York, New York 10020

This Simon Spotlight edition May 2019

Copyright © 2019 by Jason Tharp

All rights reserved, including the right of reproduction in whole or in part in any form.

SIMON SPOTLIGHT, READY-TO-READ, and colophon are registered trademarks of Simon & Schuster, Inc.

For information about special discounts for bulk purchases, please contact Simon & Schuster Special Sales at 1-866-506-1949 or business@simonandschuster.com.

Manufactured in the United States of America 0319 LAK

10 9 8 7 6 5 4 3 2 1

Library of Congress Cataloging-in-Publication Data

Names: Tharp, Jason, author, illustrator.

Title: Kiwi cannot reach! / written and illustrated by Jason Tharp.

Description: New York : Simon Spotlight, 2019. | Series: Ready-to-read |

Summary: "Kiwi sees a rope. He wants to pull it, but he cannot reach! What will happen next? Beginning readers can help Kiwi by turning the pages, shaking the book, and more in this interactive story"—Provided by publisher.

Identifiers: LCCN 2019005404 | ISBN 9781534425118 (pbk) |

ISBN 9781534425125 (hc) | ISBN 9781534425132 (eBook)

Subjects: | CYAC: Determination (Personality trait)—Fiction. | Kiwis—Fiction. | Humorous stories. | BISAC: JUVENILE FICTION / Readers / Beginner. | JUVENILE FICTION / Humorous Stories. | JUVENILE FICTION / Animals / Birds.

Classification: LCC PZ7.1.T4473 Kiw 2019 | DDC [E]—dc23

LC record available at https://lccn.loc.gov/2019005404

Maybe I can pull it
if I jump really high.

You will?
Great! I have a plan.
All you have to do is push
this launch button.

Can you help me get down? Try shaking the book up and down.

Do not worry.
I am not giving up
on that rope.
I bet this cannon
will do the trick!

Uh-oh.

Maybe it is time to give up.
At least I found this log to sit on.

BOING!

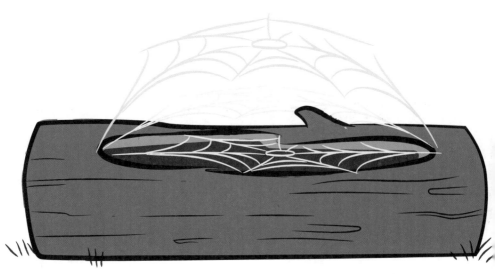

Hooray!
I am pulling the rope!
I am so glad we tried
one more time.

We did it!